A FRIEND LIKE PIKACHU!

By Rachel Chlebowski

A GOLDEN BOOK • NEW YORK

© 2019 The Pokémon Company International. © 1995–2019 Nintendo / Creatures Inc. / GAME FREAK inc. TM, ®, and character names are trademarks of Nintendo. Published in the United States by Golden Books, an imprint of Random House Children's Books, a division of Penguin Random House LLC, 1745 Broadway, New York, NY 10019, and in Canada by Penguin Random House Canada Limited, Toronto. Golden Books, A Golden Book, A Little Golden Book, the G colophon, and the distinctive gold spine are registered trademarks of Penguin Random House LLC.
rhcbooks.com
Educators and librarians, for a variety of teaching tools, visit us at RHTeachersLibrarians.com
ISBN 978-1-9848-4817-8
Printed in the United States of America
10 9 8 7 6 5 4 3 2 1

I'm **ASH**, and this is **PIKACHU**.
   In the beginning, Pikachu wouldn't do anything I asked it to. But now we're best buddies, and Pikachu helps me be a better Pokémon Trainer.

Pikachu is tough, like **BULBASAUR**,

fierce, like **CHARMANDER,**

and fast, like **SQUIRTLE.**

Pikachu is always by my side,
fighting hard!

Pikachu is loyal, like **GROWLITHE,**

and dedicated, like **JIGGLYPUFF!**

Look how cute and cuddly Pikachu and **TOGEPI** are!

Pikachu is clever, like **MEOWTH**. It can outsmart Team Rocket again and again.

Pikachu is caring,
like **BLISSEY**.

Pikachu is popular—
like **LILLIPUP**, the
Puppy Pokémon!

WINGULL helps people find Pokémon,

just like Pikachu helps me!

Pikachu can be shy, like **FLYGON**,

but when
there is trouble,
it can be brave,
like **SCIZOR**!

There is no problem too
big for my small partner,
PIKACHU!

Pikachu can glide through the air, like
EMOLGA, the Sky Squirrel Pokémon.

Pikachu is often playful, like **PANCHAM**!

Watch out!

Pikachu is energetic, like **RIOLU**.

CARBINK and Pikachu sparkle—
but Pikachu sparkles with *lightning*!

Pikachu can be sneaky, like **ROWLET**,

and stubborn, like **LITTEN**,

but it is also hardworking,
like **POPPLIO**!

Just like **MIMIKYU**, Pikachu wants
to make friends.

Hello, Mimikyu!

Sometimes Pikachu gets sleepy, like **KOMALA**.

Most important of all, Pikachu is there for me when I need it. That's why I will always choose Pikachu, my best friend!